Kiviko

TUNA FISH TUESDAY

Look for more of
doug & mike's Strange Kid Chronicles:

#1 *Mighty Monday Madness*

#2 *Tuna Fish Tuesday*

Coming soon to a bookstore near you:

#3 *Wisenheimer Wednesday*

. . . but don't look for anything else because we haven't written anything else yet. Duh.

DOUG & MIKE'S STRANGE KID CHRONICLES

TUNA FISH TUESDAY

AN
APPLE
PAPERBACK

SCHOLASTIC INC.
New York Toronto London Auckland Sydney

ISBN 0-590-05955-6

12 11 10 9 8 7 6 5 4 3 2 1   7 8 9/9 0 1 2/0

Printed in the U.S.A.   40
First Scholastic printing, November 1997

dedicated to God.

When Doug isn't talking about himself in 3rd person, he's making video games. His next game is titled "SkullMonkeys." Doug owns a Tamagachi and also likes to swim.

dedicated to my dear friend Tammy.

Mike is terrible at playing video games and doesn't have a pet Tamagachi, but ironically designs and illustrates many video game boxes. Mike has a daughter that just turned one, he's shaping a surfboard for her birthday.

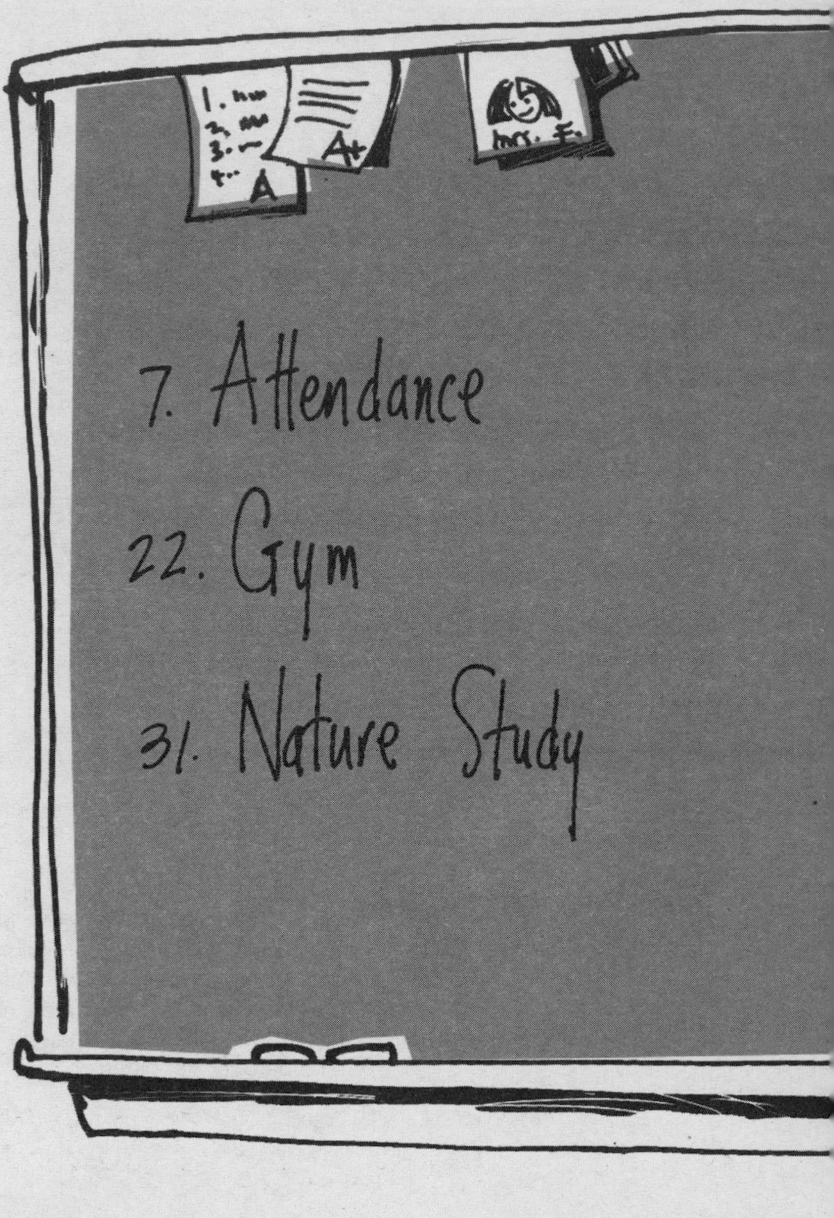

A
A+
Mrs. F.
7. Attendance
22. Gym
31. Nature Study

Mrs. Frightenright
44. Reading
52. Art
63. Dismissal
Quiz after lunch
_ o s _ r

YIPPEE!!! It's Tuesday and man, are you gonna freak when you find out what happens today in Mrs. Frightenright's class.

Welcome to doug & mike's Strange Kid Chronicles, where anything can happen on an average school day in a not-so-average classroom. Let's see, today we've got giant ants, a kid who is constantly picking his nose, and Clockboy the mechanical mystery!

Pretty cool . . . Very tempting . . .
I dare you not to turn the page.

I DARE YOU!

Boy, that was easy. We didn't even have to

DOUBLE DOG DARE YOU!

BEST FRIENDS

Doug O'Dork and Mikey Mold were walking to school. Mikey picked his nose and said, "Hey, Doug, how did you get such a giant chocolate stain on your shirt?"

Doug looked down at the brown blotch and said, "It's not chocolate."

Mikey said, "Oh."

They jumped off a curb and splashed in the sewer on their way across the street. Doug stomped a few drops of sewer water on Mikey's bright-white socks. Mikey got mad and said, "Hey, dude! Watch the splashing! I told my mom I'd make it through the whole day without getting dirt on my socks."

"Sorry, man," Doug said apologetically.

Suddenly a big yellow school bus drove by and splashed a giant wave of water on Mikey Mold. He was drenched in brown and green water from head to knee. Luckily, his socks were missed entirely so his mom would still be proud that he kept them clean!

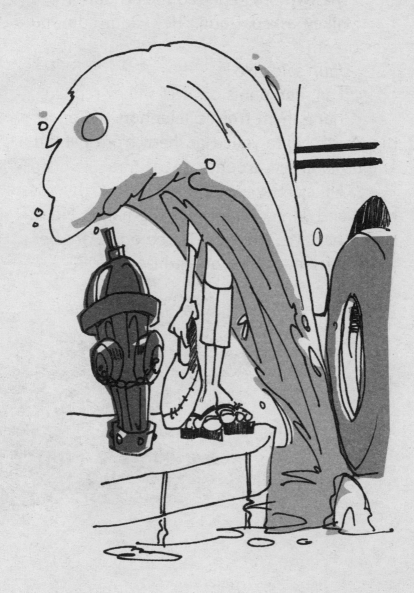

The two boys entered the schoolyard.

Mikey asked Doug, "Hey, Doug, do you ever dream?"

Doug said, "No."

"Lair, liar, pants on fire!" Mikey replied.

"Hang them from a telephone wire . . .!" Big Mouth Moira yelled to them from behind. The boys turned around.

"Mikey! Hey, Mikey and Doug." It was Moira and Jared the pig holding hands. Moira closed her eyes and said, "Jared and I are better best friends than you and Doug!"

Mikey Mold rolled his eyes. He hated it when Moira bragged!

Mikey said, "You and Jared are worst enemies compared to me and Doug!"

"Doug and I," Doug said.

Mikey turned to Doug, "Hey, dude, you're always correcting my grammar!"

Doug said, "That's because you talk like an ignoramious!"

Mikey poked Doug on his stained chest and said, "Who are you calling an '**iguana**mous'?!"

Doug and Mikey started whacking each other on the head with their books when Moira gloated, "See? Jared and I are much better best friends than you two. Ha, ha!"

Moira and Jared skipped off to Mrs. Frightenright's class.

Doug and Mikey felt pretty stupid.

"Me sorry." Mikey said.

Doug was about to correct Mikey when he stopped himself and said, "I'm sorry, too."

Doug and Mikey entered Mrs. Frightenright's class the better bestest friends in the world.

ATTENDANCE

It was Tuesday and children poured into Mrs. Frightenright's classroom like soup. The noise they made entering the room was horrendous, shattering several house windows across the country. Spencer said, "Hey, barf-bag you just sat on my lunch sack!"

Flying Vera yelled back, "Hey,

barf-sack you just sat on my lunch bag!"

Big Mouth Moira asked, "Who stole my lucky pen?" I'm nothing without my lucky pen. Oh, here it is . . . in my hand."

Peter Darch and Weird Ellis were sharing stories about the day before.

Peter said, "Yesterday I played with my inside-out dog when I got home from school."

Ellis said, "Really? When I got home from school I played with my two-headed cat." Weird Ellis then added, "Hey Peter, I now see you're stuffing steamed carrots down your pants."

Peter replied, "Yeah, we ran out of brussels sprouts."

"Fine choice, my friend," Ellis continued.

Everyone was chatting with one another except for Clockboy. He wound up alone, face and hands blue from the cold, crisp morning.

"Where is Mrs. Frightenright? We need her to turn on the heater. I'm freezing!" Flying Vera said with a shiver.

"Weird Ellis answered, "She isn't here yet."

"How do you know?" Vera asked.

"Because her hot rod of a car is not in the parking lot yet!" Ellis laughed.

Just then a horrible, thunderous sound roared around the street corner. It was Mrs. Frightenright in her backfiring red-hot '59 Ford.

VROOOM!

it went as she pulled into the parking lot. She hurriedly parked the beast next to the bike racks, got out, and ran to the class apologizing, "I'm so sorry for being late!"

"That's okay, Mrs. Frightenright," Clockboy said.

Carlos piped in, "No, it is not 'okay'! Our tax dollars pay for her time, and she should be here at eight o'clock sharp!"

"Give it a rest," Clockboy said, as he passed his homework to the front of the class

for Mrs. Frightenright to collect.

"Everyone get to your seats. We have to take attendance quickly to make up for my tardiness!" Mrs. Frightenright said as she turned on the heater.

Mrs. Frightenright was about to turn to sit at her desk when the classroom door slammed open. Eerie organ music played as Principal Prickly-Pear entered the room. **He stunk.** Weird Ellis held his nose and waved his other hand in the air saying, **"Silent, but deadly!"**

Meanwhile, Clockboy looked around trying to hear where the music was coming from. The principal was huffing and puffing from carrying a heavy wooden crate.

"Oh!" Mrs. Frightenright said as she opened up the classroom windows, "You surprised us, Principal Prickly-Pear!"

He stood there wearing a slimy smile and the tackiest plaid suit you ever saw. Moira giggled to Jared, "Now THAT'S a fashion don't!"

"Good Morning, Mrs. Frightenright. I have a new student for you. He transferred in from an undiscovered island in the South Pacific," Principal Prickly-Pear said.

Mrs. Frightenright sweetly asked, "Where is the boy?"

Principal Prickly-Pear dabbed his forehead with a slimy black handkerchief and sneered, "He's in the box."

"A box is no place for a boy!" Mrs. Frightenright said as she turned and noticed that Prickly-Pear was slinking out of the classroom in a hurry. The door closed behind him and the class suddenly smelled a little better.

The class just stared at the wooden crate. Mrs. Frightenright wanted to set a good example, so she brightened up and said, "Who will help me figure out how to open this?"

Clockboy suggested, "I believe you will use the letter-opener on your desk to pry the boards off."

Mrs. Frightenright said, "Well, that's worth a try."

She picked up her letter-opener and had only popped two of the boards off the top when a wild creature leaped out of the box and stuck to the ceiling.

The class jumped back. The thing on the ceiling stared down at the class with two giant, lemon like eyes. Everyone felt the urge to look away from the thing's haunting gaze.

Weird Ellis said, "I've never seen one of those before!"

"What in the world is it?!" Carlos asked in complete terror.

Ellis said, "It's got a lot of matted hair."

"Yeah, but so does Doug O'Dork!" Moira said.

Carlos continued, ". . . and it has big pointy teeth!"

"Like Moira!" Doug yelled.

Ellis said, ". . . and those claws! They could tear into one of us with ease and bring us to an untimely death!"

Mrs. Frightenright said, "That's enough! This is not a THING! This is a fine young child whom we will treat with respect!"

"Me not child. Me THING!" a voice from somewhere said.

"Nice grammar," Doug said.

The class followed the voice and realized

it was coming from the creature on the ceiling.

"Excuse me. Did you say that you were a THING?" Mrs. Frightenright asked.

"My name is Thing!" he gurgled.

"Welcome to the class, Thing. Would you like to take a seat behind Jared?" Mrs. Frightenright asked.

Jared began to sweat like a pig, "Oh great! He's going to sit behind me . . . then eat me!"

Moira tried to encourage him, "Don't be silly, you'll be fine!"

Jared grew cross and yelled, "Oh! Easy for you to say! You sit in front of me! Why don't the two of us trade places if it's so safe?!"

"Are you crazy?" Moira laughed, "And get eaten by Thing? No way!!!"

Jared put his head in his hands, "I'm doomed."

Then Thing spoke, "Thing no like sitting in chairs. Thing want to stay on ceiling."

Jared looked to Mrs. Frightenright, hoping she would let Thing stay on the ceiling.

"Okay, Thing, you may stay up there," she said.

Jared jumped on his desk and did the hula singing,

"I can't stop shakin'
He don't like bacon!
Unless he's fakin'
For goodness sakin'!"

"That's quite enough, Jared," Mrs. Frightenright said as Jared took his seat. Mrs. Frightenright opened the top drawer of her desk and pulled out the class roll book and took attendance.

Meanwhile, Thing noticed that when he looked down at the class from the ceiling he saw lots of cool shapes. If he squinted his eyes just right he could see an elephant on a

what do you see?!

rocketship. On the other side of the class he could just barely make out an apatosaurus wearing a chef's hat. He thought he saw the shape of a pig, then realized it WAS a pig.

Jared felt Thing's gaze and looked up at him nervously.

"He's got those 'make me into bacon' eyes!" Jared gulped. Thing had no such desire. If anything, he would rather try to make tasty sausages.

Thing then looked up at the ceiling. He saw all kinds of stuff stuck in the light fixtures where nobody could reach. He started knocking them all down. Flying discs, rubber bands, pencils, gum, tennis balls, paper clips, hairbrushes and a rare baseball card from 1972 flew here and there. As the free stuff rained down, the class erupted in cheers.

"Hooray for Thing!" some yelled.

"Hey, I didn't get anything!" Jared squealed.

Mrs. Frightenright said, "You see class, Thing can reach just about anything. He can even change our light bulbs without a ladder!"

Thing then found a dozen donuts that were at least two years old. Everyone in class wanted them. Thing walked down the wall and crawled along the floor with the box of donuts under his arm. Thing went straight to Jared's desk. Jared was so nervous that he was shivering as he broke out in a sweat. Thing came even closer to Jared. The class grew silent. The only sound was the ticking of the clock. Thing placed the box of donuts on Jared's desk and jumped back up to the ceiling. Jared looked up at Thing. Then he looked down at the box and ate all twelve in two bites.

It was time for the class to line up for Physical Education with Mr. Oxygen. Everyone lined up, including Thing, who crawled down from the ceiling. The class marched out to the front of the gym. Mr. Oxygen waited with a bunch of football equipment. On the field stood a team from another school who came over to play a game. Mr. Oxygen said, "Everyone put a rag in your pocket! We're going to play flag football!

The class from the other school was full of the biggest kids Mr. Oxygen had ever seen. The other team's coach was named Mr. Blitzer. Mr. Blitzer crossed his arms and bragged to Mr. Oxygen, "My class will completely demolish your class at football."

Mr. Oxygen's class had played Mr. Blitzer's class for ten years straight, and Mr. Blitzer's class won every time. The two teams were ready to go. Lining up for the first play, Weird Ellis looked up and saw the kid he had to block. This kid was a MONSTER. Ellis figured that one of his parents had to be a tractor. As a matter of fact, each kid from Mr. Blitzer's team looked similar to large metal machinery.

Thing hiked the ball to Brian Armstrong. Weird Ellis ran down the field and waited for the football to be thrown to him. Nose-pick Neil was the only player wide open to receive the ball, so Brian Armstrong threw the ball toward Neil.

If Neil caught this ball his team would score the first touchdown! The ball spun in the air and both teams scrambled to catch it. The ball was out of everyone's reach . . . except for Neil's. But Neil's finger was up his nose. (This is not the best position for catching a ball. You should always use two hands.) You see, Neil

loved to pick his nose. Wherever Neil was, whether in the playground, at home, at school, or in church, he insisted on keeping one finger up his nose. In fact, no one had ever seen that one finger. Due to his nose-picking routine, it forced him to do everything with one hand. This required a lot of practice. But he was able to tie his shoe, ride his bike, and even feed his dog . . . all with one-handed finesse. Kids laughed at him constantly. This didn't stop Neil from picking his nose.

Mr. Oxygen looked at Neil disappointedly. "Neil," he said, "Get that finger out of your nose!"

"You've got one more chance, Neil. If you miss the next pass I will come over there and pull that finger out of your nose for you!" Mr. Oxygen screamed.

Both teams lined up again, and Mr. Oxygen glared at Neil as he continued to pick his nose. Mr. Blitzer looked over at Mr. Oxygen and gave him a big smile. Neil wanted to pull his finger out of his nose, but he couldn't.

The reason why Neil picked his nose, unknown to everyone, was that there was a teeny, tiny city living on the tip of his finger. If this tiny city ever saw the light of day, it would disappear. The mayor of this city sat around a table with the other townsfolk who lived on the tip of Neil's finger. They wanted Neil to catch the next pass. If he didn't, Mr. Oxygen would surely pull Neil's finger out of his nose, destroying their city with daylight.

The mayor of the teeny, tiny city cleared his throat and spoke, "If Neil keeps his finger in his nose he will never catch the football!"

The mayor's lovely and enchanting secretary cleared her beautiful throat to speak. The whole town watched as she curled he antennae just right, blinking he long eyelashes, exclaiming, "We have to make sure that Neil catches this next pass!"

The crowd agreed, nodding their heads and clapping. Then the mayor asked, "But how will we do it?"

The game went on for an hour and both teams had scored many touchdowns. Mr. Oxygen:s team was just one point ahead. Thing hiked the ball again, and both teams pushed and pulled at each other so that no one was in the clear to catch a ball. Suddenly, Neil broke free and ran as fast as he could away from the crowd of players. If Neil could score a touchdown, it would put his team ahead by a mile.

Armstrong cocked his arm back as he spotted Neil way beyond the tangle of players in front of him. Brian Armstrong fired the football like a cannon, and it spun in a perfect spiral toward Neil. Neil stood in the endzone, ready to catch the ball to score a touchdown.

Neil concentrated on the ball as it floated down to his expecting arm. Mr. Oxygen screamed, "Neil, catch that ball with two hands or you'll stay after class and do eight hundred push-ups!"

Chill, Neil thought.

Neil didn't understand what the big emergency was if his team was already winning. But despite this, Neil felt his legs shaking in his cleats.

Both teams eagerly watched as the ball fell into Neil's hand. His fingers tried to tighten around the ball, but it was too big. As the ball hopped out of his hand, Neil reached forward, hoping to catch it before it hit the ground. He grabbed the lace,

and the ball bopped Neil in the face,

tumbled across his chest,

and twirled over his knuckles

just before it hit the ground. Neil put his head down in shame as Mr. Oxygen ran toward him screaming. Neil knew that he was going to have to take his finger out of his nose, and the entire city of tiny people would be destroyed.

Suddenly Big Mouth Moira yelled, "You're at the wrong side of the field, you moron!"

Mr. Oxygen then realized that if Neil had caught the ball, he would have scored a touchdown for the other team and lost the game! "Neil! You just dropped the ball and won the game for us!" Mr. Oxygen shouted out with glee.

Neil was a hero. In honor of the historical victory, Mr. Oxygen put his finger up his nose and said, "Neil, all of us should spend a little more time with our fingers up our noses!"

NATURE STUDY

The class returned from gym with Neil riding on their shoulders. Mrs. Frightenright waited for everyone to settle down. All the kids sat at attention with one finger up their nose. She began, "First let's all thoroughly wash our hands, and then we have a special treat for nature study."

A light thumping could be heard as Mrs. Frightenright continued, "Today, it is such a pleasure to introduce to you a group of special ants. They only come out of their cave every five hundred years and they are with us today."

Ellis said, "I have an **aunt** that only comes out of her cave every five years!"

The class erupted in laughter. Mrs. Frightenright said, "No, Ellis, I'm talking about the insect!"

"Oh! You mean **ants**!" Ellis said.

"Yes!" Mrs. Frightenright said.

"What about **uncles**?" Ellis asked, and the class laughed loudly again.

Mrs. Frightenright said, "Let's all give a warm welcome to the giant ants."

The classroom window broke and a bunch of giant black ants crawled into the classroom. The class cheered as one of the ants said, "Thank you, thank you. It's a pleasure to be here. Now, for no particular reason,

we'd like to smell all of you."

The ants stood there and looked at the students. Then they started to lightly tap their antennae on things they wanted to "smell." Another ant crawled in from the window. He made a beeline for Mrs. Frightenright and tapped his antennae on top of her head. It looked like he was playing bongos on her hair. *This is peculiar behavior for guests,* Mrs. Frightenright thought.

Meanwhile, all of the kids giggled. Mrs. Frightenright smiled at the big ant and it stepped back down to the floor. Another ant walked carrying a brand new computer. "Yee-haw! Now we can play computer games all day!" Doug O'Dork said. The ants set the computer down on a table and plugged it in with his giant pincers.

Mrs. Frightenright asked, "Class, what do we say to the nice giant ants for bringing us a computer?"

The class answered in unison, "Thank you, giant ants!"

"Thank you, giant ants!"

"Thank you, giant ants!"

Mrs. Frightenright then asked the ants if they could sit still so she could give the children a science lesson on "The Ant."

"Look children, we can study the ants up close without the use of a microscope!" Mrs. Frightenright said as she pointed to the biggest ant's head, "This is the head."

Then she pointed to the middle section of the ant, "This is the thorax."

The ant giggled. He was a bit ticklish. Then she pointed to the tail end of the giant ant, "And who knows what this is?"

Jared raised his hand. "The butt?"

The class roared laughing. Mrs. Frightenright made Jared stand in the corner.

She said, "The tail of an insect is called the abdomen."

"These ants are better looking than my aunt!" Ellis said.

Moira said, "Ape dung is better looking than your aunt!"

Mrs. Frightenright wondered what else the ants had scheduled for their class visit. She turned to the ant with a red spot on its head and asked, "What would you ants like to do today?"

The ants all walked over to the chalkboard and one of them gently gripped a piece of chalk in its jaws.

"They came to eat all of our chalk!" Flying Vera yelled.

"No, look! It's writing!" Peter said.

Sure enough, the ant was using the chalk in his mouth to mark on the board.

When the ant stepped away, the marks on the chalkboard looked just like a game of hangman. The ant looked back to the class like he was waiting for someone to guess. Brian Armstrong raised his enormous hand. The ant nodded to him.

Brian said, "Is there an 'A'?"

The ant shook his head no as he turned and began writing on the board.

His head was so big that the students had to wait for him to move it out of the way before they could see what he had drawn. The class was amazed at what they saw . . . a stickman's head drawn in chalk.

"Looks like today is a big day for stickmen," Clockboy said.

Everyone in the class wanted to give the next guess, so they all quietly raised their hands. The big ant walked between the rows of desks and the kids whispered, "Pick me! Pick me!"

Neil whispered in a nasal voice,"Pick me!"

Mikey Mold said to Neil, "You already pick you!"

The ant nodded at Truman, the Hairiest Kid in the World. Truman guessed, "Is there an ?"

The ant walked back to the chalkboard, claws tapping across the tile floor. He scribbled on the board a little and when he stepped away, the class saw that the last spot in the five-space word had an "E" on it.

Before long a "U" was correctly guessed by Neil (He thought of this letter because his dog was named "Ugene"!) Then Jared thought of a cupcake.

"C?" Jared guessed.

An "L" was guessed by Mrs. Frightenright.

Good answer!
Good answer!

the kids sang in agreement.

Doug O'Dork was begging, "Oooh! Ooh! Pick me! Ooh!"

The ant picked Doug. Doug sat there with a puzzled look on his face and said, "I forgot what I was gonna guess."

Clockboy guessed the final letter, an "N."
The word was

"UNCLE."

"These ants have a great sense of humor!" Mrs. Frightenright said. The class clapped their hands and cheered. They were all screaming for another round of hangman. But instead, one by one, the giant ants took a bow and left the classroom. They looked sad. The ants knew that they could not come back for another five hundred years.

Cindy begged, "Oh please don't go!"

The last ant walked up to Mrs. Frightenright and whispered in her ear. Mrs. Frightenright smiled and whispered back to him. The ant nodded and Mrs. Frightenright stood up and cleared her throat.

"Ahem. We now have a new student in the class." she said.

The class cheered.

Mrs. Frightenright announced, "His name is Grant and he wants to stay and learn how to speak, read, and write like the rest of us!"

"Grant the Ant! That's very cool!" Jared said. Grant sat behind Jared, immediately smelling the pig with his antennae. Then, Mrs. Frightenright gave him a book and a pencil.

Grant helped the class with all kinds of things. Because he could lift twenty times his own weight, he often gave the whole class rides during recess. His jaws also worked great as a pencil sharpener. Soon all of the class wanted to sharpen their pencils in Grant the Ant's mouth instead of the real sharpener in the room.

READING

Clockboy never looked at the clock in the classroom, nor did he wear a watch. But he still always seemed to know what time it was. Some said that his head was full of gears and springs like a Swiss watch. When Clockboy was born, many doctors and scientists came over to his house and looked in his ear to see the machinery that moved in there. He had a round face and pointy hands.

Clockboy's heart made a ticking sound. A bell went off in his head every morning to wake him up.

Clockboy was not only made up of clock parts, but he was also able to time travel. Clockboy could easily move back and forth into the past, present, or future. Clockboy liked the present the best so that's where he mostly stays.

One day, Flying Vera misspelled the word Tuesday like this: "Teusday." Yes, like many kids she switched the U and the E. (Of course, I'm sure all of our readers are much too smart to misspell Teusday.) Clockboy looked at Flying Vera's paper and said, "You know, today may be Tuesday for you, but it can be Friday for me if I want it to be."

Flying Vera laughed and said, "Clockboy, you're nuttier than a candybar with nuts!"

Clockboy's face and hands moved in a mechanical fashion as he gestured, "Well, laugh if you must, but right now as I look into the future, I can see you in Friday and you are screaming for help."

Flying Vera challenged him, "Prove it, Clockboy!"

Clockboy rolled up his sleeves and held his hands up over his head. At this point the whole class was watching him. Clockboy reached out in front of him and his arms disappeared into a fold in the air.

"I'm reaching into Friday right now." Clockboy announced.

He grunted as he pulled, and then he jerked a perfect copy of Flying Vera out of Friday! This copy was identical to Tuesday's Flying Vera, but there was one difference. Friday's Flying Vera was covered in slimy octopus tentacles and screaming like a baby.

"Get this gunk off of me!" Friday's Vera screamed.

Tuesday's Flying Vera dropped her mouth open and just stared at herself from the future. Clockboy pulled the tentacles off of

Friday's Flying Vera and threw them, through a fold of air, back into Friday. Clockboy said, "Okay. Today's Flying Vera should be called 'Tuesday Vera' and Friday's Flying Vera should be called 'Friday Vera'."

Tuesday Vera said, "I don't like this. You should put Friday Vera back, Clockboy!"

Friday Vera screamed, "No! Don't put me back into Friday. I was being eaten by an alien with giant tentacles!"

Clockboy covered her mouth and said, "You can't tell the rest of the class about the future! If you can't keep your mouth shut, I'll put you back into Friday."

The class screamed,

"TELL US ABOUT FRIDAY, VERA! TELL US WHAT WILL HAPPEN!"

Clockboy grabbed Friday Vera by the hand and said, "I must put you back in Friday, Vera, but I'll make sure I put you back in a safe place!"

Tuesday Vera said, "Good-bye, Friday Vera, you sure are a good-looking girl."

Clockboy stuck his hands into a fold in the air. He said, "Don't worry, class, I am reaching into Friday and putting her in a place where those creepy tentacles can't find her."

Just before Friday Vera disappeared she said, "Thank you, Clockboy! You saved my life."

Flying Tuesday Vera walked up to Clockboy, "You're right, Clockboy, you can see the future."

"Well then, Clockboy," Carlos began rubbing his hands together greedily. "Will I win my baseball game this Saterday?!"

Clockboy said, "Before I tell you, let us

first talk about your spelling of Saturday."

Then the class started to bombard Clockboy with all kinds of questions about the future.

"Will my cybernetic eyeball kit arrive in the mail soon?" Weird Ellis asked.

Mrs. Frightenright interrupted, "That's enough! We will learn about the future when it gets here!"

The class settled back down. Mrs. Frightenright handed out large sheets of paper to every kid in the room. She said, "Everyone take out your crayons. It's time for art."

Cindy could not find her crayons. The rest of the class was quietly drawing their favorite pictures. Mikey Mold drew a picture of a cat with a unicorn horn. "I made a 'uni-cat'!" Mikey said.

Grant the Ant drew with

four of his hands
at the same time. Cindy saw
the other kids were having fun drawing, but
she needed to get some crayons. Weird Ellis
got up to show Mrs. Frightenright his drawing
of a ghost so, while he was busy, Cindy decid-
ed to use his crayons without even asking
for his permission. Cindy grabbed his
newest-looking crayons, the ones with the
sharpest points, out of Ellis's crayon box.

She couldn't draw people very well so she drew a giant stickman. Meanwhile, Mrs. Frightenright admired Ellis's art, "Ooooo, that's a great ghost Ellis."

Ghost →

Ellis proudly marched back to his seat when he noticed that Cindy was using his stuff. He looked at what Cindy was drawing and grew terrified. "You didn't use one of my **absolutely incredible mysterious crayons** did you?" Ellis asked.

Cindy growled back,

"Yeah, I used one of your dumb old crayons. So what?!"

Ellis yelled back, "You knucklehead! Those are **absolutely incredible MAGICAL crayons**!!! Even I don't use them!"

Just when Cindy was about to stick the crayon up Ellis's nose, her paper began to vibrate. Suddenly her stickman drawing jumped off the paper! Cindy couldn't believe what she was seeing. Mrs Frightenright stood up in her chair and whispered to herself, "Sometimes this class . . ."

The giant stickman danced on top of Ellis's desk. The class thought it was funny until the stickman grabbed Moira's crayon and scribbled all over her portrait of Jared.

Moira yelled, "Hey! That crazy stick-man drew a stinking mustache on my picture of Jared!"

Jared looked over at the drawing and said, "I'm a good-looking pig, even with a mustache!"

The stickman was breaking kids' crayons and throwing erasers at them. The naughty stickman put a piece of gum in his mouth and after chewing it for a few seconds, spit it into Truman's hair!

Cindy knew this whole mess was her fault, so she came up with a plan to stop the stickman. Cindy looked through Ellis's mysterious crayon box again where she had found the **absolutely incredible mysterious crayons**. But, this time, she pulled out the **absolutely incredible mysterious eraser**! When the stickman ran by her desk again, Cindy erased one of his legs. The stickman was not used to running with only one leg, so he fell flat on his face. The kids in the class laughed at the stickman. The stickman grew angry until his face turned red. Then he chased Cindy around the room on one leg. He couldn't hop after her fast enough, of course, but Cindy was getting tired of running, and the stickman did not look as if he was going to stop anytime soon.

Then Weird Ellis had an idea. He laid a large piece of paper on the floor. Weird Ellis stuck out his leg and tripped the stickman as he chased Cindy. The stickman landed flat on the piece of paper that Ellis had laid out for him. The stickman lifted his face off of the paper and there was an ugly scowl. Man, he was mad! Before he could get up, Cindy grabbed an **absolutely incredible mysterious crayon** and drew a big box around him on the piece of paper. Then she wrote the word:

"JAIL"

above the box. The angry stickman tried to get out of the drawn box, but he couldn't.

The whole class was so happy to see him trapped that they all worked together to roll up the piece of paper with the boxed stickman on it. Mrs. Frightenright taped the roll up so that it could not come apart. Cindy put the roll in the corner and yelled at it, "You were such a bad stickman that you will stand in the corner forever!"

Mrs. Frightenright said, "Cindy, I think you also need to spend some time in the corner until you learn to respect other people's property."

"Yes, Mrs. Frightenright," Cindy said as she dragged herself back to the corner next to the roll of paper. Cindy looked into the tube of paper and saw the stickman look up at her and stick out his tongue.

DISMISSAL

The dismissal school bell rang. Mrs. Frightenright excused the kids. During the commotion, as the children scurried out of the classroom, Principal Prickly-Pear scurried in and quickly took a seat. The buses came, the

children went home, and Mrs. Frightenright noticed that Principal Prickly-Pear was sitting in the back of her classroom. "Principal Prickly-Pear, I didn't see you come in." she said.

"I need some paper to draw a chart in my office!" he hissed.

Mrs. Frightenright said, "Let me get you some right over--"

"I'll just take this!" he interrupted as he grabbed the roll of paper that held the sinister stickman drawing.

Mrs. Frightenright tried to warn him, "But that has a --"

Principal Prickly-Pear shook his fist and said, "Don't try to change my mind about my chart! I intend to use it to clearly illustrate what a bad job you are doing as a teacher!"

He rushed out of the room with the paper coiled under his arm.

Mrs. Frightenright just smiled.

Bonus Pages

Can you find out what the mystery character is
by connecting the dots?

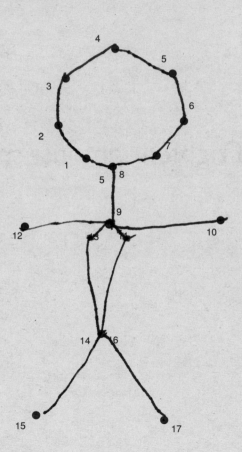

Bonus Pages

Use this page to draw your own magical stick-man or any of the other crazy characters of doug & mike's Strange Kid Chronicles.

Beware, for tomorrow is

Wednesday!

Are you scared of what that day will bring? Well, you should be! Here's a peek at what's in store for Mrs. Frightenright's class . . .

See **you** in class tomorrow!